WITHDRAWN

Any dog knows that two bones are better than one—but not when one of them is only a reflection in a pool....

Young children will want to tell their own stories about the dog who frolics through the pages of this playful wordless picture book.

THE OTHER BONE

ED YOUNG

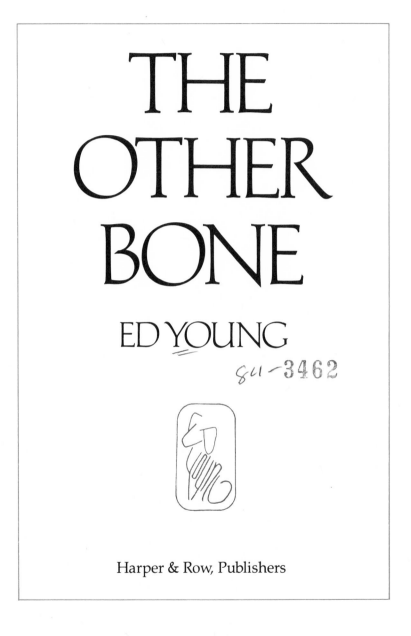

Harper & Row, Publishers

Library of Congress Cataloging in Publication Data
Young, Ed.
   The other bone.

   Summary: A dog loses his bone when he volleys with
his own reflection in a pool.
   [1. Dogs—Fiction.   2. Stories without words]
I. Title.
PZ7.Y8550t 1984   [E]   83-47706
ISBN 0-06-026870-0
ISBN 0-06-026871-9 (lib. bdg.)

1   2   3   4   5   6   7   8   9   10
First Edition

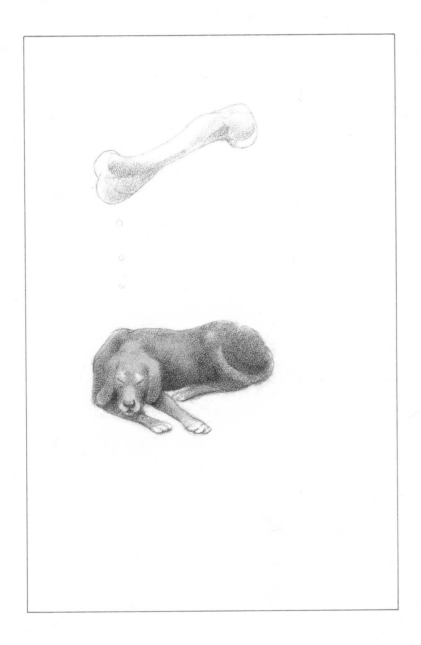

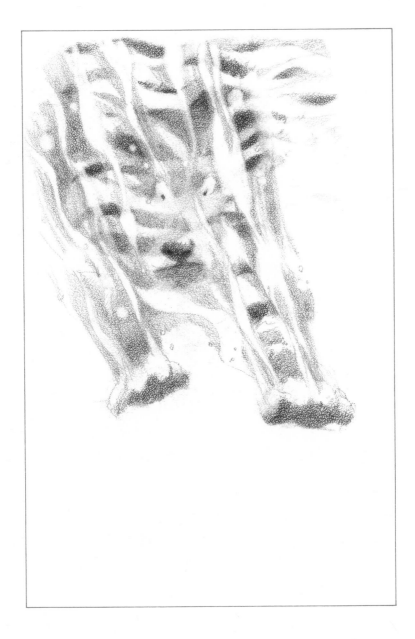